12/24/12

GO
BACK
TO BED!

BY GINGER FOGLESONG GUY

ILLUSTRATIONS BY JAMES BERNARDIN

 Carolrhoda Books, Inc. / Minneapolis

Carolrhoda Books, Inc.
A division of Lerner Publishing Group
241 First Avenue North
Minneapolis, MN 55401 U.S.A.

Website address: www.lernerbooks.com

Library of Congress Cataloging-in-Publication Data

Guy, Ginger Foglesong.
    Go back to bed! / by Ginger Foglesong Guy ; illustrations by James Bernardin.
        p.   cm.
    Summary: Every time Edwin is sent to bed, he creeps back downstairs and
discovers wondrous events going on there.
    ISBN-13: 978–1–57505–750–7 (lib. bdg. : alk. paper)
    ISBN-10: 1–57505–750–6 (lib. bdg. : alk. paper)
    [1. Bedtime—Fiction. 2. Imagination—Fiction. 3. Stories in rhyme.]
    I. Bernardin, James, ill. II. Title.
    PZ8.3.G9645Goab 2006
    [E]—dc22   2005015002

Manufactured in the United States of America
1 2 3 4 5 6 – JR – 11 10 09 08 07 06

For my nieces and nephews:
the big ones, the little ones
—G.F.G.

To my two Edwins,
Wyeth and Bryson, with love
—J.B.

"Sleep tight," said Daddy.
"Sweet dreams," Mama said.
But Edwin Dupree frowned
and pleaded instead.

"Can't I stay up?
Just a little bit more?"

"NO, Edwin," said Mama,
closing the door.

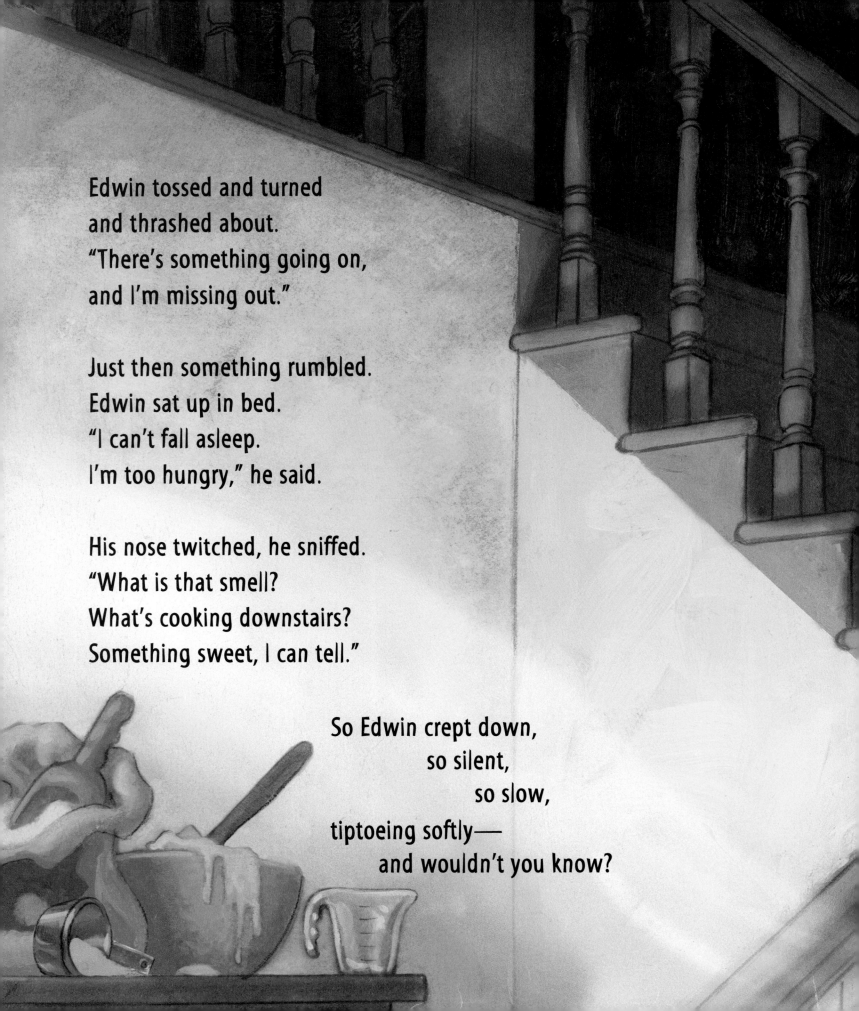

Edwin tossed and turned
and thrashed about.
"There's something going on,
and I'm missing out."

Just then something rumbled.
Edwin sat up in bed.
"I can't fall asleep.
I'm too hungry," he said.

His nose twitched, he sniffed.
"What is that smell?
What's cooking downstairs?
Something sweet, I can tell."

So Edwin crept down,
so silent,
so slow,
tiptoeing softly—
and wouldn't you know?

Strawberry cream puffs, tarts, and pies,
cakes and cookies and chocolate surprise!

"This cake tastes delicious! This pudding's just right!
Let's eat sugar cookies and stay up all night!"

"Go back to bed, Edwin.
Lie quiet, lie still.
You'll sleep better
now that you've eaten your fill."

Dragging his feet,
Edwin trudged back to bed.
"I'd much rather eat.
I'm not tired," he said.

Under the covers,
he lay wide awake.
"I can't wait till morning.
How long will it take?"

He pulled off his blanket
and sat up in bed.
"I can't fall asleep.
It's too stuffy," he said.

From somewhere downstairs
came a cool, gentle breeze.
"I'm roasting up here.
I'd much rather freeze."

So Edwin crept down,
            so silent,
                so slow,
tiptoeing softly—
            and wouldn't you know?

An igloo, a walrus,
mountains of snow.
Bobsledding penguins
lined up in a row!

"Look!" Edwin shouted.
"The living room's white!
Let's build a big snowman
and stay up all night!"

"Go back to bed, Edwin!
It would be best
to open the window
so that you can rest."

Sliding his feet,
Edwin slipped back to bed.
"I'd much rather play.
I'm not tired," he said.

Edwin tossed and turned and thrashed about.
"There's something going on, and I'm missing out."

He coughed a few times and sat up in bed.
"I can't fall asleep. I'm too thirsty," he said.

"What's gurgling? What's splashing? A fountain, I think.
I'll just go downstairs and get something to drink."

So Edwin crept down,
                so silent,
                        so slow,
        tiptoeing softly—
                and wouldn't you know?

Whirlpools and waterfalls, rapids that roar,
rushing and gushing and splashing the floor!

"Jump into my raft and hold on tight!
Let's drink lemonade and stay up all night!"

"GO BACK TO BED, EDWIN!

Your thirst must be quenched.
And change your pajamas,
now that they're drenched."

Then sloshing his feet,
he splashed back to bed.
"I'd much rather swim.
I'm not tired," he said.

Under the covers, he lay wide awake.
"I can't wait till morning. How long will it take?"

Crossing his arms, he sat up in bed.
"I can't fall asleep. I'm too lonesome," he said.
"My pillow's too big, the mattress too wide.
Something is missing here at my side.
Where is my bear? He's not here with me.
He must be downstairs. I'll just go and see."

So Edwin crept down,
                    so silent,
                              so slow,
          tiptoeing softly—
                    and wouldn't you know?

A deep silent forest, a flickering light,
a dusting of stars, a hoot owl in flight.

Edwin walked through the woods,
the moon all aglow,
and called out softly, "Where did you go?"

"Oh, there you are, Bear!
You don't have to be brave.
You need me. You can't sleep
alone in this cave.

"I'll tell you a story,"
he said to his bear.
And hiding a yawn,
Edwin walked up the stairs.

"I'll tuck you in bed and turn out the light.
But I am not tired. I'll stay up all night."

Under the covers, he watched the moon rise.
And holding his bear, Edwin closed his eyes.

"Sleep tight," whispered Daddy.
"Sweet dreams," Mama said
to Edwin Dupree, fast asleep in his bed.